THE MOON OVER STAR

BY *Dianna Hutts Aston*

PICTURES BY *Jerry Pinkney*

Dial Books for Young Readers

DIAL BOOKS FOR YOUNG READERS

A division of Penguin Young Readers Group * Published by The Penguin Group * Penguin Group (USA) Inc.,
375 Hudson Street, New York, NY 10014, U.S.A. * Penguin Group (Canada), 90 Eglinton Avenue East, Suite 700, Toronto, Ontario,
Canada M4P 2Y3 (a division of Pearson Penguin Canada Inc.) * Penguin Books Ltd, 80 Strand, London WC2R 0RL, England * Penguin Ireland,
25 St. Stephen's Green, Dublin 2, Ireland (a division of Penguin Books Ltd) * Penguin Group (Australia), 250 Camberwell Road, Camberwell,
Victoria 3124, Australia (a division of Pearson Australia Group Pty Ltd) * Penguin Books India Pvt Ltd, 11 Community Centre, Panchsheel Park,
New Delhi - 110 017, India * Penguin Group (NZ), 67 Apollo Drive, Rosedale, North Shore 0632, New Zealand (a division of Pearson New Zealand Ltd)
* Penguin Books (South Africa) (Pty) Ltd, 24 Sturdee Avenue, Rosebank, Johannesburg 2196, South Africa * Penguin Books Ltd, Registered Offices:
80 Strand, London WC2R 0RL, England

Library of Congress Cataloging-in-Publication Data
Aston, Dianna Hutts.
The moon over Star / by Dianna Hutts Aston ; pictures by Jerry Pinkney.
p. cm.
Summary: On her family's farm in the town of Star, eight-year-old Mae eagerly follows the progress of the 1969 Apollo 11 flight and
moon landing and dreams that she might one day be an astronaut, too.
ISBN: 978-0-8037-3107-3
1. Apollo 11 (Spacecraft)—Juvenile fiction. [1. Apollo 11 (Spacecraft)—Fiction. 2. Space flight to the moon—Fiction.
3. Farm life—Fiction. 4. African Americans—Fiction.] I. Pinkney, Jerry, ill. II. Title.
PZ7.A8483Moo 2008 [E]—dc22 2007050703

The full-color artwork was prepared using graphite, ink, and watercolor on paper.

To my daughter, Elizabeth Rose Aston —DHA

*To my wife Gloria Jean, my bright star,
and in memory of my mother, Williemae, my moon* —JP

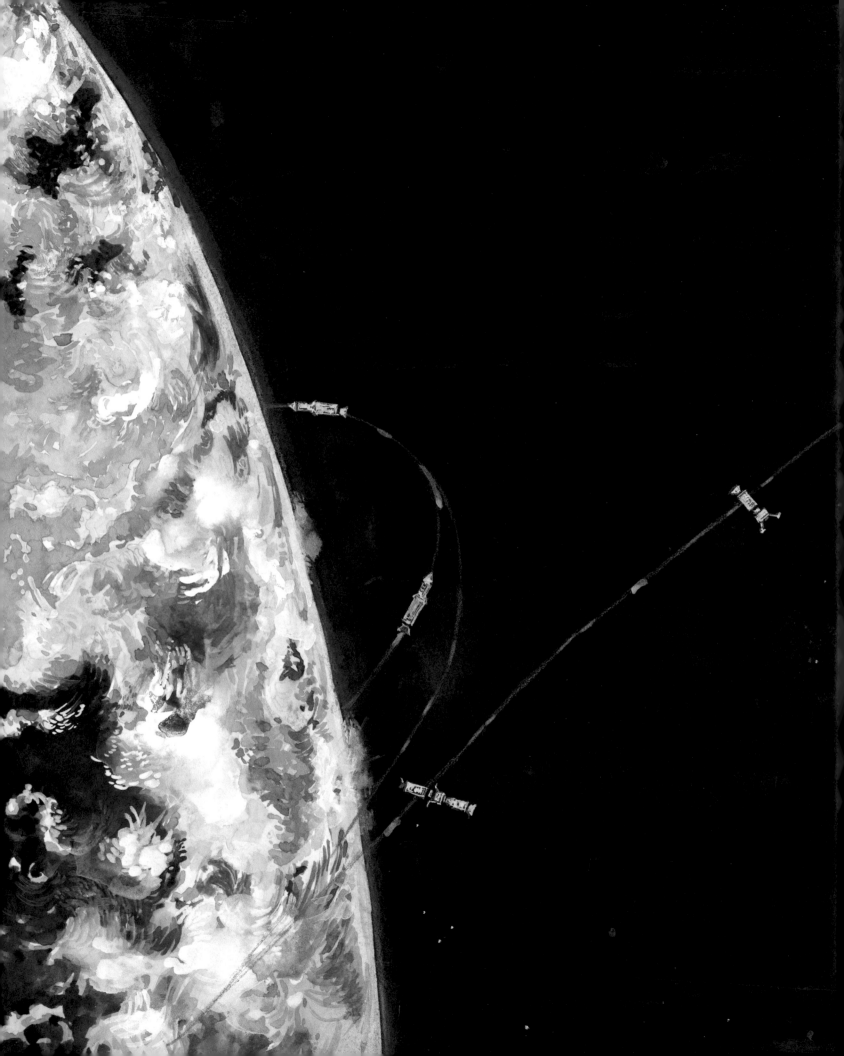

Once upon a summer's morning,

In 1969,

Grandpa led the singing in church,

The light of Sunday gleaming on his silvery head.

Through the open windows our voices sailed

Over Star, our town.

Then we bowed our heads and prayed for

The astronauts,

Neil Armstrong,

Edwin Aldrin, Jr.,

And Michael Collins.

If all went well

A spaceship would land on the moon today,

And I dreamed that maybe one day,

I could go to the moon too.

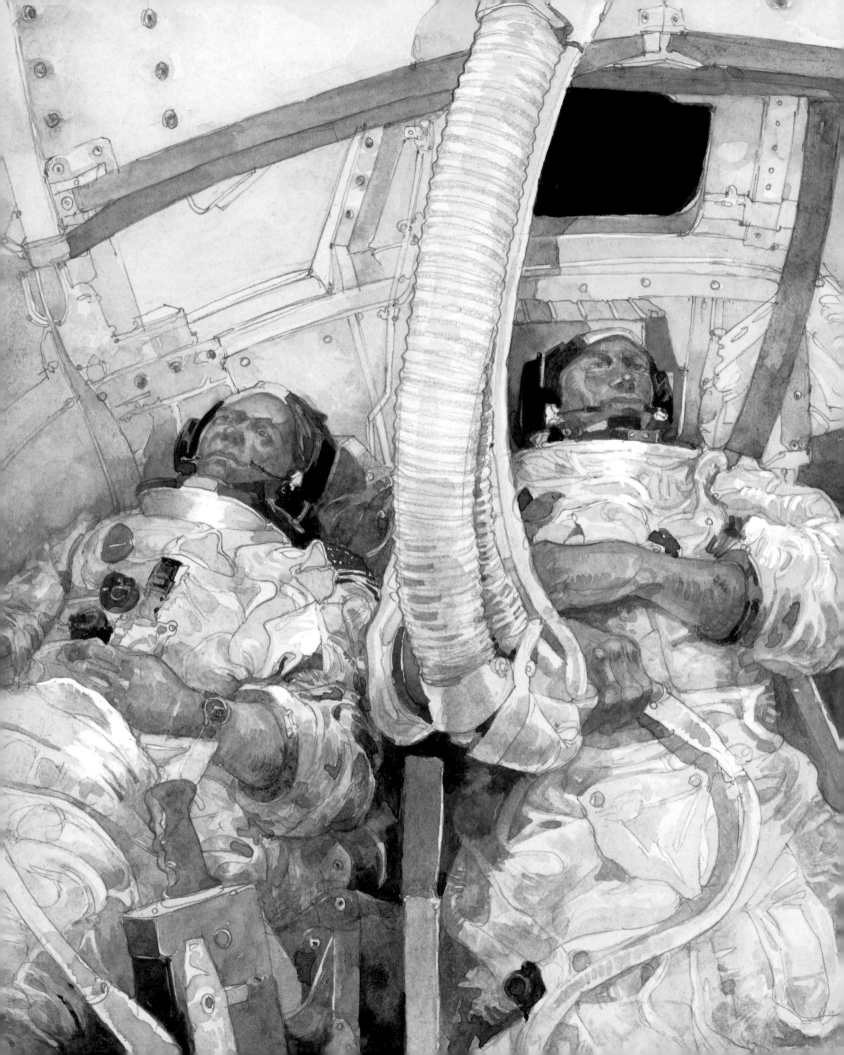

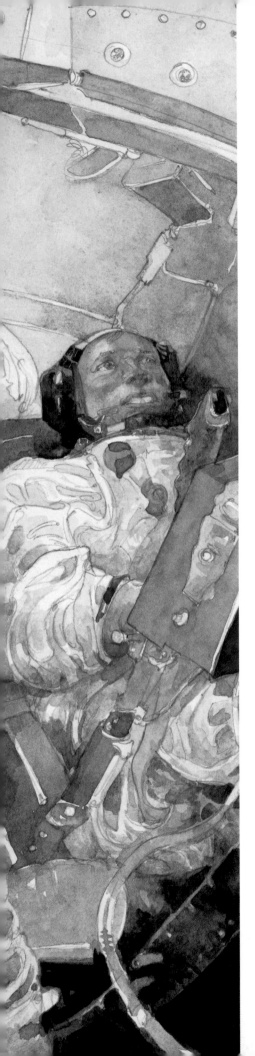

My gramps thought the space program was a waste of money,

But I knew he was praying for them too.

I thought about the astronauts' kids

And wondered if they were scared

—scared but proud.

I know I'd be. I slipped my hand into my dad's and

Whispered so only I could hear,

"God, please bless the astronauts' children too."

Once upon a summer's noon,

My cousins and I scouted Gran's watermelon patch

For the biggest one.

It took three of us to carry it to a tub of ice—three and a half,

Counting my littlest cousin, Lacey.

We decorated the picnic table with pails of wildflowers.

Then, our chores done,

We built our own spaceship

From scraps we found in the barn.

"T minus 15 seconds . . . 12, 11, 10, 9 . . ."

As the oldest grandchild, I got to be launch controller

And Commander Armstrong.

"Ignition sequence start . . . 6, 5, 4, 3, 2, 1, 0.

Liftoff, we have liftoff!"

We closed our eyes,

Imagining with all our might

The rumble, the roar, and the force

Of the Saturn rocket,

Blasting the spaceship into the stars.

Then we were rushing through space

At 25,000 miles per hour.

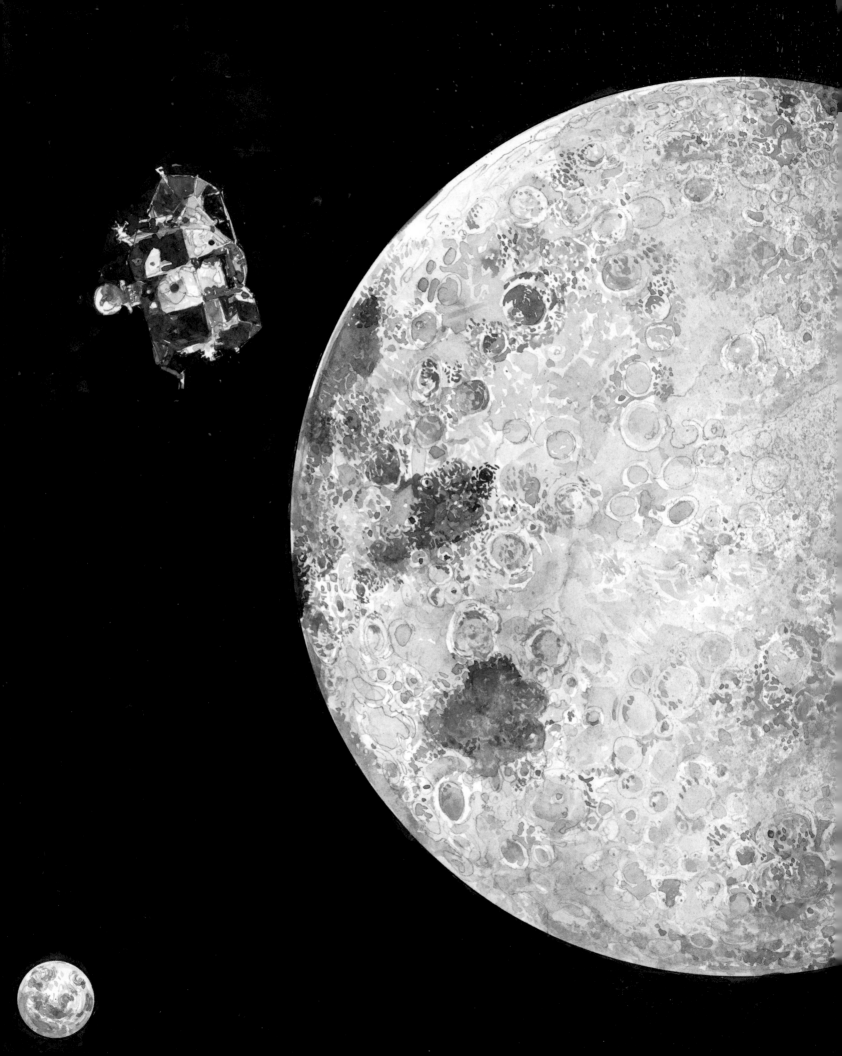

"I wonder how many miles it is to the moon," Cousin Carrie said.

I'd been reading the moon stories in the paper, so I knew.

"About 240,000 miles," I said. "And some scientists say

It's moving away from us—an inch or so farther every year."

I also knew that in May 1961,

A month before I was born,

President John F. Kennedy had said

America would send men to the moon

Before the decade was out.

Now that President Kennedy was in heaven,

I wondered if he could see the astronauts.

Was he smiling to know his dream

Was about to come true?

That afternoon,

We were helping Gramps with the tractor

When Gran hollered,

"Come quick! They're landing!"

Gramps kept right on tinkering with the engine.

The rest of us ran pell-mell for the house

And squirmed around the television screen

As it glowed

With equal parts of moon

And the spaceship called *Eagle*.

We heard the voice of Commander Armstrong

Directing the landing.

"Forward . . . forward," he said.

Then the newsman we all knew, Walter Cronkite,

Exclaimed, "Man on the moon!"

For a split second we were silent—

The whole universe must have been—

As we waited . . . waited . . .

Waited to hear the voice of an astronaut 240,000 miles away.

And then:

"Houston, Tranquility Base here," Commander Armstrong said.

"The *Eagle* has landed."

Boy, did we cheer, all of the cousins

And even the grown-ups—all except Gramps.

I remembered something he'd once said:

"Why spend all that money to go to the moon

When there's so many folks in need right here on Earth?"

"Because we can!" I'd almost shouted, but caught myself.

I began to wonder then what Gramps's

Dreams had been.

From the time he was little,

He had worked the farm,

Doing the same jobs,

Day to day,

Season to season.

When the crickets began to sing,

Gramps took out his pipe.

I pulled off his dirt-caked boots for him and

Stomped around the porch.

"Gramps, will you watch it with me tonight . . . the moon walk?"

"I'm mighty worn out today," he said, "but maybe."

Suddenly, I could see how tired he was.

Lifetime-tired.

There were deep lines in his face—a farmer's face,

An old farmer's face.

"All right, Gramps," I said. "It's okay."

Once upon a summer's night

In 1969,

We spread blankets and folding chairs

On the edge of the yard,

Where the buffalo grass grew thick and soft.

The cornstalks whispered while we

Gazed at the pearly slice of moon,

And the stars, gleaming like spilled sugar.

What were the astronauts seeing,

Right at this very second?

Could they see beyond the moon,

To Mars or Neptune or Jupiter?

We passed around a bowl of popcorn.

What I could see above me,

And what I could see in my imagination,

Were better than any picture show.

Later on that summer's night,

In 1969,

The television screen flashed with words that gave me goose bumps:

LIVE FROM THE SURFACE OF THE MOON.

And Mr. Cronkite said, ". . . Neil Armstrong,

Thirty-eight-year-old American,

Standing on the surface of the moon

On this July twentieth, nineteen hundred and sixty-nine!"

I didn't know it then, but there were 600 million people

The world over watching with me,

And listening, when Commander Armstrong said,

"That's one small step for man, one giant leap for mankind."

All of us—from New York to Tokyo to Paris to Cairo . . .

To Star—

And maybe even President Kennedy too—

All of us watched it together,

The astronauts bounding across the moon

Like ghosts on a trampoline.

I felt a hand on my shoulder.

"I reckon that's something to remember," Gramps said quietly.

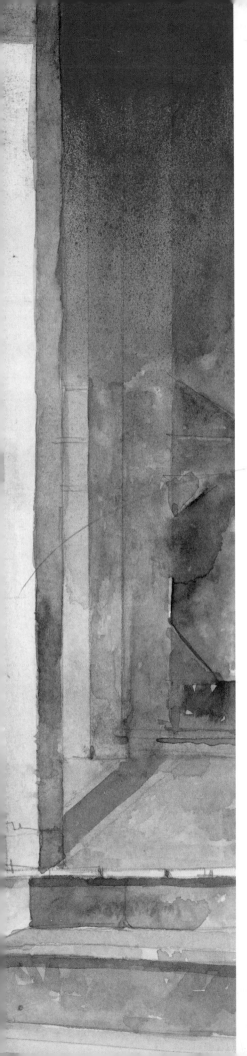

Later, when it was as quiet as the world ever gets,

Gramps and I stood together under the moon.

"What's mankind?" I asked him.

He puffed on his pipe. "It's all of us," he finally said.

"All of us who've ever lived, all of us still to come."

I put my hand in his.

"Just think, Gramps: If they could go to the moon,

Maybe one day I could too!"

"Great days," he said, "an astronaut in the family. Who'd a thought."

I smiled in the dark. My gramps was proud of me.

"First airplane I ever saw . . . I was your age . . . was right over yonder,"

Gramps said, nodding toward the cornfield.

"That was something to see, oh boy . . . something to see."

A sigh in Gramps's voice

Made my heart squeeze.

"Keep on dreaming, Mae," he said. "Just remember,

We're here now together

On the prettiest star in the heavens."

Gramps had looked to the moon all of his life.

It told him when to plant and when to harvest.

And once upon a summer's night,

It told me to dream.